This book belongs to

....

Sparkle town fairies

Alice the Amber Fairy

and the Showstopper Spectacular

Sarah Creese * Lara Ede

make
believe
ideas

In **Sparkle Town,** for all to see,
there stood a dazzling store
full of **amber instruments,**
and with a **singing** door!

Main Street

Chief Creator of things to play,
for every kind of sound,

was **Alice** the **Amber Fairy** —
the best inventor around!

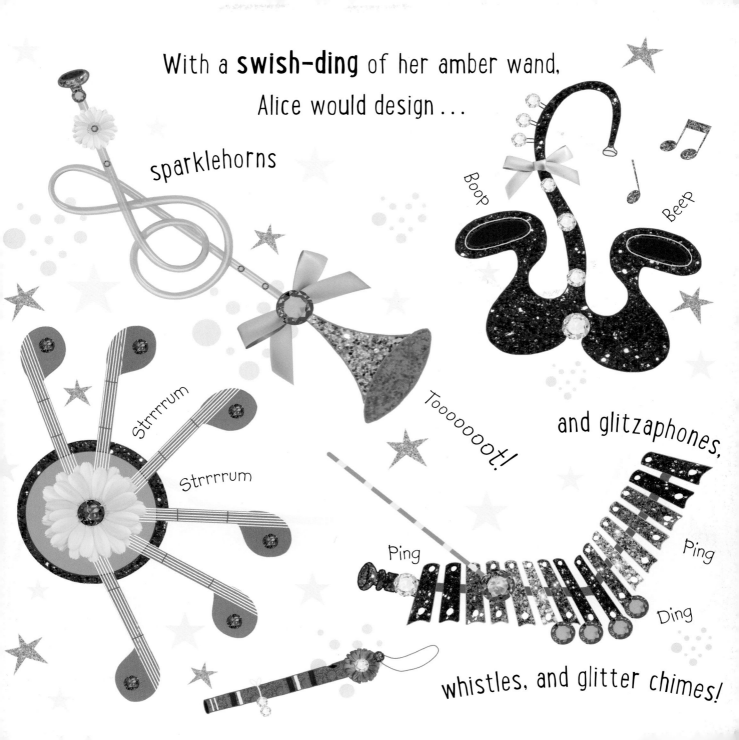

With a **swish-ding** of her amber wand,
Alice would design . . .

sparklehorns

Boop

Beep

Strrrrum

Strrrrum

Tooooooot!

and glitzaphones,

Ping

Ping

Ding

whistles, and glitter chimes!

Every **ten years** in Fairy Land,
a contest came to town
to choose a **fairy winner** for
the SHOWSTOPPER SPECTACULAR crown.

Main Street

Dear Fairies,

We proudly present the

SHOWSTOPPER SPECTACULAR

Fairy Land's greatest musical contest!

All tuneful entries will be welcomed,
but only **one** will be worthy of winning the **crown**.

Yours sincerely

Juno Jewel

SHOWSTOPPER SPECTACULAR Head Judge

It's Showstopper time!

The **Amber family** fairies had won year in, year out.

Alyssa Amber

Alfie Amber

Annie Amber

Alex Amber

Astra Amber

Amelia Amber

Amy Amber

The Ambers are musical masters!

So Alice's friends thought she would win —
of this, they had no doubt.

Ava Amber

Albert Amber

Agnes Amber

Amber Family Trophies

You're sure to win.

The **problem** was, poor Alice
(please promise you won't tell)
could not play **ANY** instrument
particularly well.

Too scared to tell her friends the truth
or let her family down,
Alice cried, "What can I do?
How will I win the crown?"

First she tried the **glitzaphone**
but her fingers were too slow,

Clink

Clunk

Me-oww!

Toot

then she tried the **sparklehorn**
but her "toots" came out too low.

The **glitter chimes**
all clashed together,

CLASH

CLANG

the bells went

ding,

dong,

wrong!

Rinnnnnng

Her **drumming** sounded too offbeat
and the cymbals rang too long!

So Alice **worked** all through the night,
inventing **more** and **more**
until she created something
unlike anything seen before...

She took a breath, then blew inside
and **without touching a key,**

the instrument played **ON ITS OWN,**

and was **TUNEFUL** as can be!

Alice practiced
"playing"
to make her
act look true
until she was
finally ready for
her **Showstopper
debut**.

As Alice watched each one perform
and play their part with pride,
she felt **guilty** about tricking them
and knew she could not lie.

Alice was called to start her piece,
and the crowd let out a cheer
(for Alice's music was the act
they most wanted to hear).

"Umm...before I start," said Alice,
"there's something I **must** say.
I'm not a good musician;
in truth, I **cannot play**.

I **created** this machine
to cover up who I am.
This instrument plays on its own;
I'm really just a **sham**."

The fairies **gasped** together. They hadn't expected that!
As Alice began to tremble, Esme appeared from the back.

Well, that was a surprise.

Oh, my!

She smiled and hugged poor Alice. "Don't feel blue," she said. "You may not be a **Showstopper**, but you're our **inventor** instead."

Alice did not play her piece,
and the **Showstopper** was won
by the most deserving fairy,
chosen by everyone.

Hurrah!

Go on, Alice!

At the **afterparty** later,
the fairies all agreed:
There was one thing that the party
did really, truly need.

They cried to Alice all at once,
"We want to hear you play!"
So Alice grinned and took a breath
and without further delay . . .

it went...

Toot-Toot, la-de-da,

BEEP and fiddle dee dee;

a-ring-a-ling, BING-BANG

oompah-ooh and WHEEEEEEE!

Though the special instrument
was **famous** near and far,

Alice learned that **best** of all
is being **who you are!**